Tap Tip Sip

Written by Caroline Green

Collins

sit in

2

sit sit

tap it

tap tap

tap tap

tap tap

7

tip it

tip tip

sip it

sip sip sip

nap in it

nap nap

13

After reading

Letters and Sounds: Phase 2

Word count: 26

Focus phonemes: /s/ /a/ /t/ /p/ /i/ /n/

Curriculum links: Understanding the world

Early learning goals: Reading: use phonic knowledge to decode regular words and read them aloud accurately

Developing fluency

- Your child may enjoy hearing you read the book.
- Read with expression to encourage your child to do the same. For example, on page 5, read **tap tap** quickly to make it sound like a tapping noise.

Phonic practice

- Turn to page 2. Point to **sit**. Ask your child to sound out the letters in each word, then blend. (s/i/t – **sit**) Repeat for page 4. (t/a/p – **tap**)
- On pages 6 and 8, ask your child to sound out **tap** and **tip**. Can they spot which letter sound is different in the words?
- Look at the "I spy sounds" pages (14–15). Point to the toucan, and say "toucan", emphasising the /t/ sound. Ask your child to find other things that start with the /t/ sound or end with the /t/ sound. (*tree, tail, tortoise, tiger, tail, eat, coconut, parrot, insect, butterfly*)

Extending vocabulary

- Take turns to read and mime the action on pages 4–5, 8–9, 10–11 and 12–13. You can then mime and mouth a word, and ask your child to guess what it is.